Alfred Allen

Australian Verse Drift; Poems

Alfred Allen

Australian Verse Drift; Poems

ISBN/EAN: 9783337206581

Printed in Europe, USA, Canada, Australia, Japan

Cover: Foto ©Andreas Hilbeck / pixelio.de

More available books at **www.hansebooks.com**

AUSTRALIAN VERSE DRIFT:

POEMS

BY

ALFRED ALLEN, OF WAVERLEY,

N. S. W.

SYDNEY :

PRINTED BY F. CUNNINGHAME AND CO.,

PITT STREET.

1883.

I Dedicate

This Little Book of Poems

TO

THE FRIENDS WHO KNOW ME.

NOTE BY THE AUTHOR.

I OFFER no apology for casting this waif on the restless ocean of public opinion; it is neither the child of affluence nor misfortune. It bears my name: I alone am responsible for its failings.

ALFRED ALLEN.

Fern Cottage,
   Waverley, N. S. Wales,
      1st Mo., 1883.

"Gie me ae spark o' Nature's fire!
That's a' the learning I desire;
Then, though I drudge through dub and mire,
  At pleugh or cart,
My muse, though hamely in attire,
  May touch the heart."

BURNS.

INDEX.

A SEA SIDE REFLECTION.

(BONDI.)

"No REST—no rest," the murmuring waves declare,
　　O'er Ocean caves they hurry on apace,
By day and night the curling billows bear
　　The one sad wail—" we have no resting place."

" No rest—no rest." Beneath the deep blue sea
　　The great stone walls are crumbling to decay,
And myriad forms work out the high decree,
　　"All Earthly things must change and pass away."

" No rest—no rest." The white sand on the shore,
　　And drifting shells exposed to wave and wind,
Among the rocks where foaming breakers pour,
　　They vainly seek a resting-place to find.

" No rest—no rest !" There is no haven here,
　　Where we may anchor shelter'd from the storm ;
'Mid sunken wrecks and dangers ever near,
　　Life's helmless bark is driven its course along.

We look for rest where all is calm—serene,
　　Where peaceful streams of living waters flow ;
'Mid waving fields of everlasting green,
　　Where shady bowers in heavenly beauty grow.

We look for rest where earthly conflicts cease,
　　Where toil and care no more with sorrow blend ;
When " dust to dust " from suffering shall release,
　　And all our longings after rest shall end.

A

THE OLD HUT.

THE old hut posts are standing yet
    Beside the mountain creek ;
And there amid the solitude
    The rubble chimney peak ;
Where many an old gum log has burned,
    In times of social mirth ;
While stockmen told their strange wild tales
    Around the open hearth.

The hewn slab floor with rugged lines,
    But always neat and clean,
Has by the flood been swept away,
    And now the grass is green,
Where gladdening sounds from baby feet
    With pleasure filled her breast,
Who long beneath that wattle shade
    Has lain in peaceful rest.

There, carved upon the grey sandstone,
    Are time-worn letters seen ;
The old sheath knife those letters traced,
    To tell that she hath been
To him the one hope of his life,
    His first love, and his bride ;
To tell to all, who stayed to read,
    The day his loved one died.

There's nothing left a stranger's eye
    Would care to rest upon ;
A roofless and deserted hut—
    A cheerless skeleton.
The little garden fence has gone,
    And ferns and thistles grow
Where once the vine and rosebush bloomed
    Just twenty years ago.

MOVE ON.

"Let me lay here quiet, and not be chived any more," falters Joe;
"and be so kind. any person as is passin' nigh where J used for to
sweep. as jist to say to Mr. Snagsby that Joe what he'd known once
is a MOVING ON right forwards with his duty, and I'll be very
thankful; I'd be more thankful than I am already, if it was any
ways possible for an unfortunate to be."—DICKENS.

THE world is going round,
The world is going round;
And everything is on the move,
Above and underground.
There's change in every sphere,
In sky, and sea, and land;
Go where we may—above—below—
There's change on every hand.

There's no such state as rest;
The sleeping rocks decay;
"Move on, move on," stern nature cries,
Upon the world's highway.
The sun, and moon, and stars,
Keep journeying on their course,
And all the heavenly bodies yield
To some unmeasured force.

All things are moving on;
They pass in grand review;
And strange, amid perpetual change,
There's nothing old or new.
No atom goes to waste;
Though lost it may appear,
It finds its place, and serves its end
On this great rolling sphere.

On! on! for ever on!
The past and present teach;
There are no boundary stones for them,
No goal for them to reach.
The Days, and Months, and Years,
March on with steady pace,
And by the one unerring law,
The worlds are swung in space.

This one unerring law
Man must himself obey,
And be the van, the foremost guard
To head the grand array.
Old science measures time,
While art and lore unite,
To aid him in his onward march,
For universal right.

TO THE SUN.

BRIGHT golden Sun! just peeping o'er the deep,
Dispersing darkness by thy herald rays;
This smiling morn to thee her homage pays,
And nature, gay, refreshed by bounteous sleep,
Dons her rich robe to meet thee, lustrous guest!
And honey'd flowers unfold their leaves to greet
Thy early kiss—while warbling songsters meet
Thy welcome step, and sing of love and rest.
We hail thy march with joy o'er plain and coast,
Thro' mountain gorge and undiscovered dells,
O'er far, far distant lands.   In ocean cells
Thy sceptre sways, and 'mid yon starry host,
And far beyond that dark and restless sea,
One unseen hand controls thy destiny.

THE POETS.

THE poets who touch the sweet chords of the lyre,
  But borrow their plumes from the classics of yore,
Workshop and cottage must fail to inspire,
  While with plumes such as these they venture to soar.

To Homer and Ovid, and Tasso, we pay
  The honor that's due to the true and the good ;
But why should the poets of every day,
  Still over these ancients incessantly brood.

Now I hail with delight the poets who teach
  Humanity lessons of kindness and love,
In sweet flowing rhyme, the pure figure of speech,
  And train them to live for the living above.

The poets who plead for the poor and oppress'd
  While they struggle mid care and sorrow and gloom,
In the battle of life yet doing their best,
  To conquer the foe on their way to the tomb.

The poets who draw from the fountain of truth,
  To comfort the hearts of the weary and worn.
And check the rash stream of the errors of youth,
  Ere down with the current the lov'd ones are borne.

Who stoop to the fallen and bid them look up,
  To silver lin'd clouds as they sail thro' the air ;
Who picture the shame in the wine-flowing cup,
  And bid the poor trav'ler of danger beware.

Who gather in wreaths sweet flowers of speech,
  For garlands to honor the true and the brave,
Who stand like the prophets of old in the breach,
  And comfort the mourners who weep by the grave.

Of such poets as these the world will not tire,
  So long as humanity groans 'neath the rod.
It will welcome with joy the heart soothing lyre,
  That leads from the world and its trials to God.

UNREQUITED LOVE.

I HAVE loved thee too well !
    Adieu, then, for ever !
My heart at love's shrine,
    Was an offering to thee.
Now I part with thy smile,
    I find we must sever ;
I pray thee forget
    All remembrance of me.

I have loved thee too well !
    My heart was a stranger
To all the devices
    Thy practised smile knew.
Those eyes might have told me
    My peace was in danger ;
So now in my grief
    I must bid thee adieu.

I have loved thee too well !
    No lover will woo thee
With love that is warmer
    Or truer than mine ;
He may win thee with wealth—
    With state ; but it may be
His truest affections
    Will never be thine.

I have loved thee too well !
    Ere I knew the keen art
By which the fair hand
    Of a maiden is gained.
Too soon I revealed
    My innermost heart,
And bade thee to look
    Where thine own image reigned

I have loved thee too well !
   The long spell is broken,
The mirage of bliss
   Is now lost to my view.
I will keep for thy sake
   The last loving token
I took from thy hand
   Ere I bade thee adieu.

OLD TIME.

THE sun has set, and soon the night
   Will fall, and close the door of day,
   Old Time will take the keys away,
And in his book the record write.

He never halts, he will not wait.
   He never stands to think awhile;
   No pleasing beauties can beguile,
He never lost by being late.

He never comes a bit too soon,
   He knows his own appointed place,
   He comes along with measur'd pace,
By night and morn and eve and noon.

His locks are grey, but not with years ;
   He never was a child in arms ;
   He's never moved by false alarms,
Nor yet by threats or smiles or tears.

He'll never pledge his word for aught,
   He wounds and cures, yet none can say,
   He favoured any in his day,
Old Time is not by favours caught.

He conquers kings, he brings to dust,
  Pain, want, and care, before him fall ;
  He brings to life, he bears the pall,
He builds the treasures of the just.

Old Time ! Old Time ! we need not fear ;
  Come lock the door, and take the keys,
  And leave us here, if thou dost please,
To meet the new and coming year.

*   *   *   *   *   *   *   *

Each rolling wave on life's great shore,
  Removes a landmark from its place ;
  The years return with steady pace
To make complete the treble score.

———————

TO A WILD ROSE IN A LETTER.

On floral wings, wild mountain-rose,
  Go—as the peaceful, sacred dove,
That left the Ark to seek repose—
  And bear the message of my love.

Clothed meekly in thy native bloom,
  Sweet emblem of a cloudless day,
Before it comes—thy hour of doom—
  Go, bear a love-thought far away.

Thy tiny form is now at rest,
  Embalm'd with thy own fragrant breath ;
No storm can reach thy tinted breast,
  Or wake thee from the sleep of death.

Thy comrade-flowers shall seek thy face,
  And grieve to find thy beauty flown ;
Some other rose will take thy place,
  But thou art mine, and mine alone.

THE STRANGER.

PART I.

'Twas early morn, and I had left
My humble cot, to wander 'mid the hills,
And in the grove I met an aged man,
Whose snow-white flowing locks and stately mien
Fill'd me with wondering awe and rev'rent love.
He had no staff, but in his hand a scroll,
Which bore the language of some foreign clime.
His garb was plain, but so unique, it seem'd
More like a robe of other days, and yet
It showed no trace of wear, nor dimm'd by age.
His head was bare, and by the morning light
I well could trace his high and archèd brow.
His eye was lit by some ethereal power;
It searched me through and through, I know not how.
My lips were sealed, I dared not venture words.

He raised his hand, then pointing to the skies,
" My friend," he said, " my country yonder lies,
But, leaving freedom for a time, I come
To visit earth again, that I may learn
What progress truth has made since last I stood
And heard Christ teach the wondering multitude.
I was a seer in my day, and scorn'd
At first the teachings of the Nazarene.
We Levites deemed they were incompetent
To lead men higher than the common rule,
Until we saw in His pure life the fruit,
And evil conquered by His passive good.
Taught by the learned rabbis of my time,
'Twas hard to know that all I'd learned was lost,
And in old age to find my treasures gone.
I could not thus submit in child-like trust
To one unlearned, who offered in return

For loyalty to Him, the loss of all,
With scourge, imprisonment, and worldly scorn—
To one of humbler birth, who in the schools
Had never sought in quest of classic lore,
Nor from the fathers learned of sacred law,
Nor e'en could trace from Levi His descent.

" But yet, withal, His mystic words did win ;
    Confident of innate power, he spoke
Of righteousness and joy and peace within,
    And bade the people bear a lawless yoke.

" I gladly joined with Pharisee and Scribe,
And in the Temple searched through ancient scroll
If I might haply find wherein He err'd,
And thus refute the common babbler's word.
In vain, in vain I tried ; all efforts failed ;
The Scriptures testified as he had said ;
New lustre shone in every written page,
And o'er me, as I read, a voice I heard,
' O, Israel ! hear through flesh the living Word.'

" Philosophers of every school of thought
Had vied to give the seething multitude
Some settled faith in which the mass might find
One common goal—a balm for every doubt ;
They vied, but vied in vain : He touched the chord,
And tuned the lyre which lay untuned so long."

The stranger paused, and drawing close his robe,
He passed me by, and soon was lost to view.
The early birds with song had filled the grove ;
I stood alone ; above, the mournful wind,
Like angels whispering, flitted through the boughs,
And, save the murmuring of the distant brook,
And bleating of the lambs, no sound was heard.

PART II.

"Here are huge walls adorned by human skill,
    With massive pillars, fonts, and spacious dome.
With classic corbel, tessellated sill,
    And trophies from forgotten Greece and Rome.

A modern Temple for the priests who seek
    The foremost place among the sons of truth,
Whose lifeless symbols feign a form, to speak
    An unknown tongue to hapless age and youth.

'Tis night, and now within this painted shrine,
    Dressed in his loose and sacerdotal cloak,
An orthodox and college-bred "divine"
    Looks from his throne of polished fretted oak.

He bows his head, and bids the people pray—
    In spirit ? No, but from the "Book of Prayer."
Then young and old submissive bend, and say,
    With ready lips, the strange things enter'd there.

The prayer is said ; the organ peals are heard,
    And with one voice the worshippers now sing ;
Another prayer ; then of the "Heavenly Word"
    The clerg'man reads, and how the seed took wing.

The Book is closed ; the Liturgy is read ;
    Another robe, and yet a higher sphere ;
The clerg'man bows again his "reverend" head,
    And supplicates the Lord to lend His ear.

And now the "sermon." Oh ! for other days,
    When He, of whom the truest preachers preach,
Who led the weary through life's troubled maze,
    And fed the hungry by El-Bathab's beach—

Who kindly taught the wayworn, burdened crowd,
  And lifted from despair the Magdalen,
And marked the silvery lining for each cloud,
  And filled the home with joy where death had been.

Oh! for his loving voice once more, to speak
  As once I heard upon Mount Olive's slope,
As He then blessed the humble, pure, and meek,
  And bade the friendless poor in Him to hope.

Within cathedral walls, 'neath spiral towers,
  Where high-toned bells ring out their merry lays,
And altars decked with marble-sculptured flowers,
  And cultured art with boundless bounty pays

Her richest tributes—oft with blood-stains wrought—
  And science yields of her rich stores the best,
And learning from the modern schools of thought
  Exalts her children—lords in knowledge dressed.

Here, but in vain, the hungry mass may seek
  The living Word on which I gladly fed;
They hear again the priestly Levite speak,
  And see the blind by blind guides being led.

They find, as then, without the fruit, the tree;
  The Temple service and the altar laid,
The sacrifice of lips—so full and free,
  And taught and teachers of the light afraid,

And agèd seers still halting as of old,
  Still scorning truth in its pure, simple guise,
Fearful, and dreading to forego their hold,
  They can but see through sacerdotal eyes.

Is this the fruit of eighteen hundred years
  Of shame and scourge, and preaching of the "Cross?"
Is this the freedom bought by martyr's tears,
  For which I reckoned all my treasures loss?"

A HYMN.

I'M weary,—oh, I'm weary
  Of life's rough, rugged road;
So cold the night, and dreary,—
  Lord! help me bear the load.
I call on Thee in weakness,
  To Thee alone I come;
And trust in Thy completeness,
  Oh! lead my spirit home.

Thou taught my feet in childhood.
  To walk in heavenly ways;
And oft-times in the wild-wood,
  Hast filled my heart with praise.
When overcome by sorrow,
  I've heard Thy loving voice
Foretell a bright to-morrow,
  And bid my soul rejoice.

When cheerless doubts assailed me,
  And fill'd my cup with grief,
And trusted friendships failed me,
  In Thee I found relief.
Oh! blessed Rock of Ages!
  Safe shelter for the lost;
Light of the ancient sages,
  And all life's tempest tossed.

I bow, O Lord, before Thee,
  And at Thy feet appear;
Oh! cast Thy shadow o'er me
  That I may feel Thee near.
I'm weary,—oh, I'm weary
  Of life's rough, rugged way;
So cold the night, and dreary,—
  Lord, hear me now I pray!

THE OTHER SHORE.

WHILE resting on my garden seat, one quiet Sabbath
eve,
Beneath a cool and shady bower where vines their
tresses weave,
My weary eyelids found a balm, an unseen hand had
pressed
So lightly on my aching brow, and bade my spirit
rest.
Asleep;—my soul by earthly ties the world no longer
held ;
It left, a time, its clay-bound home (some unseen force
impelled),
Till with the light-winged cherubims and friends of
byegone days
I met to sing with spirit-voice my early songs of
praise,—
I met to greet forgotten smiles, to feel the fond
embrace,
To see the calm seraphic peace beam in each angel
face.
Familiar strains of music fell so sweetly on the air,
And 'mid that happy, joyous throng I found no trace
of care.
I watched their strange ethereal forms and marked
their graceful mien ;
Their life was one harmonious whole of blessedness
serene.
But yet I felt I had no share in their unsullied joy ;
My garment wore an earthly hue, and bore the clay
alloy.
I could not tell what brought me there or how I
entered in,
I felt they knew I still retained a consciousness of sin ;

But yet withal I did not fear among that ransomed
throng,
I knew they were too kind to chide, too kind to do me
wrong.
They knew full well from whence I came, but pity
never breathed ;
They told me death—kind messsenger ;—had each from
earth relieved,
That o'er yon bright horizon line they watched Time's
surging foam,
For every wave that reached that line brought some
new spirit home.
" Hadst thou been borne on yonder sea," I heard a
loved voice say,
" We would have met thee on the beach to guide thee
on thy way,
A loving band would welcome thee ; thy friends who
crossed before
Would lead the host to greet thy step upon the heavenly
shore.
Abide thy time, be kind and true, the messenger will
come,
He has thy name, we'll hear it read in this Elysium.
Thy visit to this world of light should teach thee not
to dread
As mortals do who fear to leave the dwellings of the
dead ;
For what are all thy lower joys compared to these
above,
And what are earthly treasures, then, beside eternal
love ?"
Her bright eyes pierced me through and through, she
smiled with love supreme,
Her hand press'd gently on my brow, and woke me
from my dream.

A DRIFTING THOUGHT.

Oh ! sure it is, the countless ills,
    That lie as thorns upon the road,
    Are here to turn our steps to God,
For perfect love our pleasure wills.

Our joys are built on simple trust,
    On all that's seen is stamp'd unrest,
    For earth's gilt treasures are at best,
But painted toys and glittering dust.

'Tis hard to find, we know not why,
    From whom the source of sadness flows,
    The purport of our many woes,
And where the springs of sorrow lie.

We sow, and reap, and harvest now,
    Buoy'd on life's expectancy,
    We doubt our own mortality,
And live and move we know not how.

We see by faith, and nothing more,
    While peering through the mystic night,
    The gilmmer of a distant light,
Amid the gloom, on yonder shore.

From shore to shore, it's but a span,
    A narrow stream alone divides.
    A vapour cloud is all that hides
Eternity itself from Man.

AUSTRALIAN WILD FLOWERS

PRESSED IN A BOOK.

DEAR mountain gems,
With slender stems,
And clad in beauty rare,
So full of grace,
When in your place,
Ye breathe the forest air.

No human skill,
Or finite will,
Could plan your varied forms,
Which yield with ease,
To every breeze,
And bend to mountain storms.

But now entomb'd,
Your beauty's doom'd
And soon must fade away ;
My heart beguiles
Your floral smiles
My pleasure to obey.

From happy bowers,
Death takes his flowers,
With cold and ruthless hand,
He may entomb,
But still they bloom,
In a bright and better land.

IN little deeds are proofs of friendship told ;
In speaking eyes the loving heart we trace ;
From gentle acts how many joys unfold
Which Time's cold hand can never quite efface ?

To Alfred Tennyson, the Poet Laureate.

(Lines suggested on reading Tennyson's
"In Memoriam.")

Oh ! gifted muse ! thy heaven-tun'd lyre
  Has moved our hearts to truth and love,
  Has raised our sympathies above,
And filled our souls with holy fire.

Thy vigorous faith in God and right ;
  Thy simple trust " that good may fall
  At last far off, at last to all,"
Reveal thy longings after light.

So many hearts shall sing these lays,
  And with the purer mind combine,
  Which here is seen to blend with thine
Until the spark becomes a blaze.

Here is a balm for mental grief,
  A solace for the heart oppress'd,
  To soothe bereavement into rest,
Till bitter mourning finds relief.

Engraven tablets waste to dust,
  But these the laurels thou hast spread,
  As records of the faithful dead,
In memory of the good and just—

They shall endure from age to age,
  For sacred truth can never die,
  Tho' long forgotten it may lie,
It claims a heavenly parentage.

THE SONG OF CHRISTMAS.

Come lay aside your sorrows, boys,
  And Christmas hail with cheer.
Come join the merry round of joys,
  They come but once a year.
      They come but once a year, my boys,
      They come but once a year.

The old homes in the fatherland
  Still ring with song and glee.
The cabin and the palace grand.
  Alike they welcome me.
      Alike they welcome me, my boys,
      Alike they welcome me.

This new-born land of sun and shade,
  To creed and caste a home ;
Where beauty dwells 'mid hill and glade,
  Beneath a cloudless dome.
      Beneath a cloudless dome, my boys,
      Beneath a cloudless dome.

Her fairest daughters hail with joy
  My warm December smile,
For I'm their merry Christmas boy,
  Their troubles to beguile.
      Their troubles to beguile, my boys,
      Their troubles to beguile.

Of holly bough and mistletoe
  You cannot boast a share,
But to Old Christmas yet you owe
  Your " Christmas bush " as fair.
      Your Christmas bush as fair, my boys,
      Your Christmas bush as fair.

So all your cares, good folk forget
    And take my ancient hand,
Be happy while you may, and let
    Me bless your sunny land.

        I'll bless your sunny land, my boys,
        I'll bless your sunny land.

"ETERNAL HOPE."

"Eternal Hope" amid the darkness beams,
    Eternal Hope!   Eternal Hope!
Dark clouds rise o'er mediæval dreams,
    And loving eyes may see the heavenly slope
Where mercy flows in endless living streams.

Eternal Life! sweet hope of endless days!
    Eternal Life!   Eternal Life!
We see afar the bright and warming rays
    Which soon must melt the long and cruel strife
And turn our fears to ceaseless songs of praise.

Eternal Hope! oh, hope of perfect rest!
    Remove the dross, remove the dross
Which has so long the spirit life oppress'd,
    And dimmed the merits of sad Calvary's cross,
Thy bright beam kindle in each longing breast.

Eternal Hope for all our suffering race,
    Oh, blessed thought! oh, blessed thought!
A share for all of universal grace,
    A share for each of hope which Christ hath brought,
And in eternal life for each a place.

AUSTRALIA.

AUSTRALIA! land where free men boast,
 Thy sun in glory never wanes,
While peaceful billows bathe thy coast,
 And mountains guard thy virgin plains.

Oh! new-born land of sun and shade;
 Oh! land of hope without a past;
Oh! land whose youth can never fade;
 The peaceful home of creed and caste.

Thy day ne'er dawns upon the slave;
 In thee no servile fear is known;
No banners for the despot wave;
 Nor tyrant holds a blood-bought throne.

No conquering lord has ever led
 His marshall'd force upon thy soil;
Nor have thy sons, Australia, shed
 The foeman's blood in search of spoil.

Thy boast is not in empires won,
 In princely towers, baronial halls;
Thy stainless glory rests upon
 A surer trust than turret walls.

Thy flocks and herds and smiling fields;
 Thy cottage homes where honest toil
Now reaps what patient labour yields,
 Assisted by thy generous soil;

Thy noble efforts to dispense
 The needed aid to art and lore,—
These—these shall form thy sure defence
 When war-proud states shall be no more.

Then, onward, in thy march, blest land ;
    Thy future glory, who can say ?
Wed righteousness with wisdom, and
    Thy greatness shall not fade away.

THE MARTYRS.

WITH measured care each age presents
    Its honors and its adulation,
In costly tombs and monuments
To special heroes of events,
    Or men of lofty station.

We reverence the martyr's claim,
    And wreathe for him a crown of glory ;
In songs of praise we sing his fame,
While history transmits his name,
    And age to age the story.

The victor who the van has led
    To free his country from oppression,
Now rests in state among the dead,
And o'er him marble garlands spread
    To tell our admiration.

But oh ! among the ranks unknown,
    Are martyr names yet unrecorded,
For whom we rear no sculptured stone ;
Their self-denying deeds alone,
    In Heaven shall be rewarded.

" Yea. rather blessed are they who hear the Word of God,
      and keep it."—LUKE ii. 28.

LORD, those who love thy voice to hear
Are never moved by servile fear,
    They trust Eternal Love ;
Their life is thine, it came from Thee,
And will return, again to be
    And dwell with Thee above.

'Tis not the creed, or mere belief,
That brings the troubled mind relief,
    And gives the weary rest ;
It is to hear Thy loving voice,
Bid the anxious soul rejoice,
    And be for ever blest.

The surging waves Thy Word obey,
The thundering clouds their homage pay
    To Thy omniscient Word ;
The dismal walls of ocean caves,
The undiscovered desert graves,
    Alike Thy voice have heard.

All nature waits to own Thy power,
The forest tree, the wayside flower,
    They own no other Lord ;
The zephyrs gently chant Thy praise,
While myriad birds return their lays
    To Thee in one accord.

O God of all, may I obey
Thy quickening Word from day to day,
    And ever waiting be ;
Give me the trained and listening ear,
That when Thy inward voice I hear
    I'll follow only Thee.

THE CHAINED EAGLE'S APPEAL.

BOUND to my perch to please the gazing crowd,
　The long dull hours are spent, from day to day ;
My pinions droop, as to a riven cloud
　My wild eye turns to catch a solar ray.

A prisoner chained to earth, I know not why ;
　I plead for naught but this, that I may soar
Beyond that cloud beneath yon clear blue sky ;
　I plead for this, and covet nothing more.

I fain would spread again these palsied wings,
　As in my youth—those happy days of yore,
To which my memory never ceasing clings ;
　But they are gone—yes, gone for evermore.

Here life is death, a dismal vacant blank ;
　A fearful dream, a pandemonium cave,
Where spectres meet to hear my fetters clank—
　I start, 'mid fear, to fall a shackled slave.

Through Adam's sin must I too suffer woe ?
　Must endless grief rack this poor bruisèd frame ?
By what just law should I my life forego,
　Since all who live from one Creator came ?

He gave to man the noblest and the best
　Of God-like powers, and placed him over all,
That every creature might through him be blest,
　But not that he should conquer to enthral.

Would he, without a murmur waive his right
　To that blest goal he ever hopes to gain ?
What passing pleasures here could tempt his sight
　His hopes to barter for a bondman's chain ?

My heaven is here ; no hopes of future bliss
　　Their soothing rays to me their comfort lend.
Man has a life beyond the grave ; but this
　　Is all to me, and here my joys must end.

Then break the bonds and set the captive free,
　　To visit vale and cliff, my mountain home ;
Oh ! let me breathe my native liberty
　　'Midst undiscover'd realms o'er ocean foam.

For He who guides the sparrow in his flight,
　　And clothes the lily in her spotless dress,
For every injured slave demands the right—
　　For every needless pang shall claim redress.

SUNDAY AMONG THE MOUNTAINS.

" I am certain that the Sabbath is not a perpetual obligation, that
it was Jewish, and passed away with Christianity, which made all
days and places holy—nevertheless, I am more and more sure, by
experience, that the reason for the observance of the Sabbath lies
deep in the everlasting necessities of human nature, and that as long
as man is man, the blessedness of keeping it, not as a day of rest
only, but as a day of spiritual rest. will never be annulled.—*Life
and Letters*, F. W. ROBERTSON."

　　FROM busy toil and care released,
　　　　Among the hills I roam,
　　And worship in old Nature's church,
　　　　Beneath her ancient dome.

　　Within this vast cathedral aisle,
　　　　The sacred anthem swells,
　　Sublimer strains than cultur'd choir,
　　　　Or consecrated bells.

The rich and poor are served alike
  Within these sacred walls,
And for the evil and the good,
  Heavenly manna falls.

No marble fonts or colour'd panes,
  Nor tablets for the dead,
No costly pews nor priestly robes
  On human weakness spread.

No learnèd creed or ritual
  To bind my soul is here,
But still a sacred joy I know,
  And feel a presence near.

I hear the truest preacher's voice
  Creating by his Word,
As on the birth of Nature's day
  The holy angels heard.

From rocky caves and sheltered groves
  Ten thousand voices raise,
In one sweet melody of song,
  A hymn of faultless praise.

In silent rapture while I wait
  The message from above,
My soul is filled and overflows,
  With strange unearthly love!

Hail! day of rest, sweet peaceful morn,
  My tuneful soul doth praise
The Giver of this hallowed time—
  This happy day of days.

WAVERLEY.

A Retrospect.

HERE memory reckons one by one
  My early years of joy and mirth ;
  For here my brightest dreams had birth
Ere life's stern battle had begun.

Here are the rocks where once my feet
  With lightness skipped from crag to crag ;
  The sandy beach and moss-bound flag
Where still the breakers wildly beat.

Here are the hills of heath and rose—
  They rudely line the rugged shore,
  And o'er them white-plumed sea birds soar,
Waiting their victims to depose.

In boyhood's sunny hours I've played
  Among these rocks and time-worn caves,
  And breasted oft the rolling waves,
And knelt with those I've loved, and prayed.

Here, borne on fancy far above
  The callings of this lower state,
  We've sojourned till the hours were late
To measure the Eternal love.

Before the dawn we've sought the grove,
  To watch the early peep of day,
  To see the waves with sunbeams play,
Before the clouds began to rove.

These rocks and hills with sheltered glen,
  And curling waves with solemn moan,
  Oft taught my spirit whence to roam,
And drew me from the haunts of men.

These rugged hills unaltered sleep,—
  If any change, I fail to see;
  Whatever change, it is in me,—
I see none in the changeless deep.

There is no spot on earth to me
  More dear, where richer charms abound,
  Than here, and in the hills around
The rock-lined glens of Waverley.

———

"TIS ALL FOR THE BEST"

'Tis all for the best, the dark clouds above thee
  May surge in the wild wind and threaten to burst ;
And friends may prove false, the friends who should
    love thee,
  But there's no need to fear, tho' all do their worst.

'Tis all for the best : take comfort in sorrow,
  For the bark that will face the storm-troubled wave,
Will meet the fair weather and sunshine to-morrow,
  Tho' the high winds at night may hopelessly rave.

'Tis all for the best : believe it, my brother ;
  Then nobly bear up, nor give way to thy grief ;
Each burden well borne will brace for another ;
  In this cheering maxim thou'lt find a relief

'Tis all for the best, for all things are working
  Out good for the man who is honest and true :
The guilty may dread the recompense lurking,
  But he need not fear who has nothing to rue.

THE MILLENNIAL AGE.

WHEN will the true Millennial Age,
　　The long-expected reign of Peace,
Life's countless ills and wrongs assuage,
　　And bid our dark forebodings cease?

When will the diverse faiths of man,
　　In one eternal union blend,
And leave to God the hidden plan
　　To which His righteous counsels tend?

When will the ruthless bigot learn,
　　That martyr's blood, like goodly seed,
Must the hundredfold return,
　　While his own faith shall run to weed?

When will the Christian law of love
　　Be throned supreme in Church and State,
And earth reflect the life above,
　　And banish every form of hate?

The world has waited—oh, how long!
　　In vain, to greet the cloudless day,
While beating back the tide of wrong,
　　And trusting for the promised ray.

But still the dark deep shades of night,
　　Obscure the visions of the seers,
And watchmen, waiting for the light,
　　Grow weary ere the dawn appears.

A POET'S REFLECTION.

THE day is spent, and now my tent
　　I pitch, and hope to find,
Of gifts the best, sweet sleep and rest
　　For weary limb and mind.

Another day has passed away,
　　Another sun has set;
How many more will set before
　　My tent shall be to let?

My lot of years well mixed with tears,
　　I know not how they've passed;
My locks, they say, are turning grey,
　　And age is coming fast.

It must be so, for well I know
　　I'm slower in the race;
And in the field I have to yield
　　To younger men my place.

"So mote it be," 'tis well for me,
　　Thus far I've journeyed on;
If poor in purse, I'm not the worse
　　For what I've undergone.

Well, after all, my wants so small
　　Have always been supplied;
I envy not another's lot,
　　With mine I'm satisfied.

I've had a fair and honest share
　　Of friendly cheer and love,
And when my lamp burned dim and damp
　　My sky was clear above.

I know no creed, and do not heed,
  What heartless bigots say ;
But bear the rod, and trust to God
  For blessings day by day.

I court the muse to teach me truths,
  Which only angels hear ;
On wings of love I soar above
  This terrestrial sphere.

A little space, some country place,
  Where heath and mosses grow ;
Where big hills rise to greet the skies,
  And mountain streamlets flow :

Be this my home, and let me roam
  A child of nature, free,
And learn each day some rural lay,
  Some sweet seraphic glee.

And when at last the mould is cast,
  This perishable sod,
Let good folks say, without display,
  He's gone to be with God.

RELIGION is not in talking,
    But in living ;
  Not in working,
    But in obeying ;
  Not in toiling,
    But in waiting ;
  Not in praying,
    But in trusting ;
  Not in mourning,
    But in rejoicing.

"LOVE'S BUT A DREAM."

Oh ! the Lover would rather clasp the fair hand,
Than all the vast treasures on sea, or on land.
Her love is the sunshine that beams on his way,
Her smile makes the darkness as bright as the day ;
The cold world may slight him, he cares not for this,
He would part e'en with life, but not with her kiss,
She is all things to him, his bliss is complete,
When he stands at the shrine to hear her repeat,
"I am thine, only thine, and trust to thy love,
Till the Angel of Death shall call me above."

    *   *   *   *   *   *   *   *

Ah ! would that the savor of love could remain
The end of life's term and love only reign.
The flower after bloom must drop its fair form,
And the calm silver sea must rise with the storm,
And the blue azure sky, at morn without cloud,
Must at eve-time put on its dark thunder shroud ;
The grass too, in springtime, looks healthy and green,
But changes in winter its beautiful sheen,
Alas ! all things change here, the friends of to-day
Like the dew of the morn must soon pass away.
Yes, 'tis hard thus to find that Love's but a dream,
And our friends after all are not what they seem.
That all our loved treasures at best are but toys,
That earth cannot offer us permanent joys.

        I have thought in my turn,
           T'were better not love,
        But wait for the meeting,
           Of lovers above.

ADVICE TO T. H.

TAUNT me not with blissful meetings
　　When the busy day is o'er,
And of gladsome infant greetings,
　　By your dove-like cottage door.

Life would be a green oasis,
　　If wives were but what they seem,
Could we see in pretty faces,
　　More than fancy's fitful dream.

Wives of many men remind us,
　　We might meet what's term'd a "shrew,"
Who without a hope might land us
　　On the coast of Timbuctoo.

Fascinating flowing tresses,
　　Studied art and style beware ;
Tinsell'd flowers and sweeping dresses,
　　Man and brother, oh, take care.

Profit by the solemn warning,
　　Adam in his day received,
Lest you wake some sunny morning,
　　Finding you have been deceived.

Some say wives are benefactors ;
　　Well, oft exception proves the rule,
One thing surely they are actors,
　　Pupils in Dame Fashion's school.

After all 'tis best to marry,
　　Face the racket and the strife ;
Time is short; don't needless tarry ;
　　Be a man, and risk a wife.

FAIRLIGHT GLEN.

(BONDI.)

'Tis but a glen, and nothing more,
'Tis but a bay, where breakers roar,
  With rocks on either side :
A sandy beach with weed and shell,
A rendezvous where mermaids dwell,
  And crabs and limpets hide.

'Tis but a wild and rugged nook,
Divided by a tumbling brook
  In search of ocean foam ;
Where melancholy finds relief,
And poets learn to measure grief,
  And listless lovers roam.

A spot where birds each other greet,
And fairies in the twilight meet,
  And lights and shadows blend ;
Where ferns and rushes grow apace,
And vines of " sweet tea " interlace.
  And gentle violets bend.

Where mountain heath and native rose
With honeysuckle find repose
  Beside the shatter'd cave :
While o'er the picturesque cascade
Tall palms afford a summer shade,
  And graceful bamboos wave.

'Tis but a glade, and nothing more,
Where day and night the deep sea's roar
  Reminds us of the past ;
Where storm and tempest lose their sway,
And murmuring zephyrs seem to say,
  The hours are flitting fast.

It is a charm for every eye,
A balm for every ache and sigh,
  And speaks of scenes above ;
Unlike the noisy crowded street
With every form of woe replete,
  This fills the soul with love.

In shore, and glen, and dwelling-place,
The muse would lead my mind to trace
  A reflex of man's state.
The sparkling stream like living truth,
The trees resemble Age and Youth ;
  And there the wicket gate.

'Tis but a nook, and nothing more ;
'Tis but a bay where breakers pour
  'Mong rocks their snowy foam ;
Where verdure smiles the season thro',
And flowers of every form and hue,
  In Fairlight find a home.

———

WRITTEN IN A BIRTHDAY TEXT BOOK.

This book with thy consent shall bear
  My love wish penn'd in broken measure,
That I with other friends may share
  A passing thought in hours of leisure.

Its border'd leaves so faintly lined
  With chosen texts from sacred pages,
And names inscribed shall bring to mind
  Friends of to-day and bygone ages.

BEYOND THE GRAVE.

[On reading that the Rev. Henry Ward Beecher had expressed his
distrust in the doctrine of " Eternal Punishment."]

BEYOND the grave, beyond the grave,
　　For those who die uncleansed from guilt,
No arms, alas ! outstretch to save,
　　No sacrificial blood is spilt.

In Hell's dark pit they ever lie,
　　The lost, consigned to endless pain ;
No mercy rays illume their sky ;
　　They dwell where taunting demons reign.

Eternal loss ! Eternal shame !
　　No hope, no change, 'mid ceaseless pangs ;
For ever tortured by the flame
　　That round the guilty spirit hangs.

　　*　　　*　　　*　　　*　　　*

Great God ! can such a doom await
　　The erring creatures thou hast made ?
Is there no goal, no far-off date,
　　When the full ransom shall be paid ?

No dispensation of thy love—
　　Redeeming by remedial pains ?
No message from the sacred dove
　　To loose the sin-bound sinner's chains ?

We trust, we fearless trust to Thee,
　　And not to blind and vengeful man ;
We know that what is just shall be,
　　And judge thee by no human plan.

Nor guess we here what hence may be,
  For those who fail man's crucial test;
We leave them, Lord our God, to Thee,
  Thou only knowest what is best.

FAREWELL.

FAREWELL! dear friend, farewell!
  The flowers that bloom
  And loving thoughts
In after days shall tell
  How I have loved thee.

New friends may come and go,
  And friendships wane—
  And time may fill
The cups of joy and woe,
  I'll not forget thee.

'Tis hard indeed to part
  With one so dear,
  But duty calls.
Still ever in my heart
  A place I'll keep thee.

The paths we oft have trod
  I'll walk alone:
  Yes, without thee;
And breathe a prayer to God
  Through life to bless thee.

And now again, Farewell!
  Submissively
  I bow to Him,
He doeth all things well.
  May angels guard thee.

HASSAN'S WALLS.

THE sky above was clear, an ether blue
Shrouded the distant hills ; and at our feet
The buttercups still held the morning dew,
And the wild " forget-me-nots," with " blue-bells,"
Bent their graceful forms to the early breeze.
Our little party, five, when numbered all,
The night before, agreed to meet and spend
The mid-day hour upon " High Hassan's Wall,"
Whose towering peaks, three thousand feet and more,
Rise from the level of the dark deep sea.
With staff in hand, and having for our guide,
One who well knew where winding paths divide.
We left the humble cot before the sun
Had journeyed far across the eastern sky.
So merrily we travelled on, we knew
No reason why the blissful hours should end,
And blithe and gay we sang and bounded on,
Till we had reached the mountain track that led,
Like " Jacob's Ladder," to bold Hassan's head.
Here we pursued the journey's heavy task,
Up steep ascent, along the mountain ridge,
Where rough huge boulders rudely interposed,
And forced our weary limbs to seek the crag
That jutted out, to form a rugged bridge—
Between the hills—thro' fragrant wattle bowers
Where "maiden-hair" and ferns of statelier mien,
Adorn the shattered caves ; and rarely peeps
A wandering solar beam, and warbling songsters tune
Their notes so wild, from early morn till eve.

    *   *   *   *   *   *   *   *

The day was just half-spent, the summit gained,
The vision opened, and proud nature spread
Ten thousand wonders to our awe-struck gaze.
West Hartley lay a speck amid the hills,

The old coach-road a grey and winding line;
And tumbling time-worn walls, fantastic shaped,
Rose from the green abyss, like hoary lords
Enthroned for judgment, o'er the silent dells;
Or stood, like marshalled sentinels, to guard
" Victoria " Mount from every lurking foe.
The mighty chasm seemed itself to charm—
To paralyse the brain by some dark spell—
By some mysterious power, so awful, grand !
Far down beneath the dreadful mountain gorge,
A hideous gulf (where Dante might have gleaned),
Sent forth no cry of woe or bitter wail ;
The mocking pheasant's note alone was heard ;
Trees, flowers, and shrubs, with hill, ravine, and glade,
Joined in the testimony of ages,
And sang aloud the handiwork of God ;
The ground, we felt, was sacred 'neath our feet,
We stood as on the lofty cliffs of Kadesh,
In God's vast Cathedral, where He alone
Is heard to speak from rolling thunder-clouds.
In reverential awe we humbly bowed
Beneath the mighty dome which spanned all space,
And inly breathed the heaven-taught prayer to Him—
That we alike in harmony might blend
With all his works—and serve His righteous end.

OLD FRIENDS.

I KNEW one little spot on earth,
Where happiness and joy and mirth
   Robb'd sorrow of its sadness,
Where love had found without alloy,
The truest peace and purest joy,
   And fill'd the place with gladness.

The visions of my untrained mind,
With all my hopes and joys combin'd
　　To give me satisfaction.
My love on earthly objects staid,
To earthly forms I homage paid,
　　And bow'd to their attraction.

I trusted that maturer life
Would be secure and free from strife,
　　Might never know deep sorrow.
The world a garden did appear,
And nothing caused my heart to fear ;
　　I car'd not for the morrow.

But potent time can disarrange,
And all our cheering prospects change,
　　And spoil us of our treasures ;
And thus we learn by constant care
To build no castles in the air,
　　Or trust to coming pleasures.

The friends I've loved I ever will,
For dear indeed to memory, still
　　To memory cannot perish ;
Like early dreams, so bright and fair,
Their love as incense in the air,
　　My heart shall ever cherish.

Death and space may long divide,
And from my view the lov'd ones hide,
　　And intercourse may sever.
Regardless of earth's boundary line,
Love soars on high to realms divine,
　　And journeys on FOR EVER.

WHAT I HAVE SEEN.

I'VE journeyed afar o'er the blue rolling wave,
    And o'er mountain and valley I've sped ;
I've sat by the mourner, when over the grave,
When looks of despair, and true sorrow were there,
    As the sods were thrown over the dead.

I have sat by the bed of the sick, when clouds
    O'er the valley so dismally hung,
I've aided to wrap the poor clay with the shrouds,
When the die has been cast, and shadows have pass'd,
    And the last mortal link has been wrung.

I have sat at the board, when spectre-like want
    Chill'd with his touch the poor scanty store,
Where poverty strode with a jeer, and a taunt,
Distressing by fears, regardless of tears,
    Made the helpless for mercy implore.

My lot has been cast, where good fortune has shed,
    All her gifts with a generous mind,
Where luxuriant wealth his bounty has spread,
In silver and gold, amid treasures untold,
    And with affluence, comfort combin'd.

I've stood by the bride on the bright nuptial morn,
    When the birds, and the flowers were gay,
When nature herself seem'd so proud to adorn,
And gave blossoms so fair, as gems for her hair,
    And thus smilingly welcom'd the day.

But yet this I have found in every clime,
    We struggle for pleasure and power,
Forgetting that life is a pilgrimage time,
Where peasant and king, from one parentage spring,
    Then fade in their turn as a flower.

THE PAST.

Oh! where are the friends of my earlier days
   Who were with me in sunshine and glee,
Who, ere I had entered the world's maddening maze,
   Were all the world could be to me ?

Oh! where are the vows we then lovingly made,
   The castles we built in the air,
The plans we together so carefully laid,
   And treasures we promised to share ?

Oh! where is the rapture that ravished my heart
   When the light shone in from above,
And bade my dark fears of a future depart,
   And filled my whole nature with love ?

Oh! where, in the depths of my sorrow, I ask,
   Can I find my once simple creed ?
Was my ignorance bliss, to folly a mask ?
   Was faith not a flower, but a weed ?

The friends of my youth here no longer remain,
   They have drifted down on the stream,
The hopes which I cherished are riven in twain—
   Have passed like a beautiful dream.

But friendships and pleasures have no settled rest,
   For time changes everything here,
And plans formed in youth are but shadows at best
   Which only in sunlight appear.

In Memoriam

THOMAS SUTCLIFFE MORT.

Oh ! youth and age your tribute pay—
　　A token of your inmost grief—
　　For death has claimed his final fief,
And spread his curtain of dismay.

Australia's prince of enterprise,
　　The man of noble life and deed ;
　　The man who taught the fearless creed,
Oh ! bid your songs immortalize.

No patriot loved his country more ;
　　He labor'd for the common good ;
　　A lover of the brotherhood :
The generous friend to art and lore.

Place in the nation's album page
　　A fadeless image of his face,
　　That so posterity may trace
The higher lines of parentage.

Let science bow before the bier,
　　And commerce walk with unshod feet,
　　And o'er the grave let strangers greet,
And shed the sympathetic tear.

Then when the burial prayer is read,
　　And one has said the " dust to dust,"
　　The world shall add, " The good and just
Now rests among the sacred dead."

THE SHADOW.

WHIRLING along on the glistening rails,
Over culvert and bridge I fly,
From my carriage window watching the forms
As they pass me hurriedly by;
But the clank of the iron wheels beneath,
And the song of the pent-up steam,
Have started my brain with wandering thoughts,
While of other days I dream.

Whirling, burling, tearing along,
Through forest trees I fly,
Over culvert and bridge,
Over river and ridge,
But I sit at the window and sigh.

A shadow travels wherever I gaze,
And anon it rests in the air,
On mountain and plain, where wild waters flow,
Wherever I turn it is there;
It skips o'er the grass, and floats in the breeze,
And follows the train in its flight,
Over tall trees like a sunbeam it darts,
And tips the wild blue-bells with light.

Whirling, burling, tearing along, &c.

It flirts with the clouds and smiles at the wind,
Like a bird on an endless wing;
But it changes not its curious form,
'Tis a vague and meaningless thing;
Through tunnel and gorge, uncheck'd in its course,
It journeys so freely at will,
Unheeding, undaunted, careless it sports,
Never touching valley or hill—

Whirling, burling, tearing, along, &c.

Oh ! shadow of death, of life, or of love,
Come tell me thy message I pray,
Break now the dark spell, relieve my sad heart,
And drive my forebodings away.
True emblem of life, of all things below,
Thy lesson with sorrow I learn.
Oh ! shadows are seen wherever I go,
But shadows wherever I turn—

     Whirling, burling, tearing, along, &c.

IMPROMPTU LINES

WRITTEN IN A LADY'S ALBUM.

SCRIBES are not uncommon,
   They're legion, nothing less,
Who practise album gammon,
   And write like letter-press.
Many a bright example,
   Within this book I find,
But here I give a sample,
   Of quite another kind.
'Twill be a pleasing contrast,
   Beside the sparkling lore,
Which friends will scatter broadcast.
   From Byron, Scott, and Moore.
Well, let the critics read it—
   Nor mince what they would say,
I hope my friends will read it,
   And to its author pay
A tribute of affection,
   And stay their righteous ire,
Should it on close inspection
   Lack warm poetic fire.

My *nom de plume* I will not give,
   That on this page my name may live.

To Thomas Gainford,

MINISTER OF THE MARINERS' CHURCH.

How many years of anxious toil and care
    Have pass'd and glided down Time's restless stream;
How many years thy life of work and prayer,
    Has been, to darkened ways, the Bethel beam.

Thy lamp has shone across the waves by night,
    And mariners upon life's surging foam
Have seen the gleam, and gloried in the light
    Which led them thro' the tempest, safely home.

If but one soul has reached yon far-off' port,
    Been saved from wreck upon the rugged coast;
If but one life is safe beside the fort,
    And anchored now among the ransomed host;

If drooping hearts o'ercome by cankering grief,
    And loveless lives, have, by thy lips, been moved;
If Thou hast given to troubled souls relief,
    And shown by whom the guilty stand approved—

Then princes well may envy thy reward;
    Their crowns before thy gem-set crown shall wane,
The "come thou blessed," spoken by thy Lord,
    Shall be to thee beyond all earthly gain.

For what are all the empty honors here?
    They surely fade as all things fade below;
They sparkle for a time, then disappear,
    But there each honor wears immortal glow.

We would not raise the curtain of the past;
    The many years of service now are sealed;
Among the varied forms their mould is cast,
    To wait the hour when all shall be revealed.

'Tis not for us to know, O Lord, how long
　Our sojourn here together may be spent ;
We simply know from Thee to us no wrong
　Can come—no dark nor unforeseen event.

––––––

BEYOND THE SEA.

(A SONG.)

HERE from the spray-worn cave,
　I watch the angry foam—
Snow-white plumes upon the wave,
　While my fancies roam
Far as thought can carry me,
Beyond the Sea ! Beyond the Sea !

Murmuring billows breathe
　Their sad, sad tales of woe,
While the breakers rudely seethe
　Among the rocks below ;
Gladly would my spirit flee
Beyond the Sea ! Beyond the Sea !

Here far from every eye,
　Communing with the past,
While before me wonders hie,
　And unseen joys forecast,
That my soul shall one day be
Beyond the Sea ! Beyond the Sea !

Here death and sorrow sway,
　And pain and pleasure blend ;
Here treasures never stay,
　And love's bright mornings end ;
But there every life is free,
Beyond the Sea ! Beyond the Sea !

THAT GLITTERING STAR.

(A SONG.)

Oh, that glittering star! That glittering star !
   I watch its flickering ray,
Up in yon shoreless space so far,
   It bears my soul away :
On land, or sea, where'er I roam,
That star shall guide my spirit home.

There's a charm in that glittering star for me,
   A secret promise of love,
A gleam no other eye can see,
   Drawing my soul above.
On land, or sea, where'er I roam,
That star shall guide my spirit home.

Oh ! that glittering star far off in the west,
   Through many a cheerless night,
Has lulled my troubled heart to rest,
   And spread my path with light ;
On land, or sea, where'er I roam,
That star shall guide my spirit home.

There's a glory around that glittering star ;
   It witness'd my early vow
Which time, nor death, can ever mar ;
   A hallow'd pledge, and now
On land or sea, where'er I roam,
That star shall guide my spirit home.

Time, like these waves upon the shore,
   Will leave no trace of earthly joys.
Our hopeful plans are nothing more
   Than shifting sands or childish toys.

"THEY ALSO SERVE WHO ONLY STAND AND WAIT."

THE evening shade the valley fills,
  And mountain tops reserve the light,
While shadows skip among the hills,
  As if to shun the coming night.

The wind moans gently thro' the trees,
  The kine return to seek repose,
And birds sail home upon the breeze,
  The day draws swiftly to its close.

A gentle maiden bathed in thought,
  With soul as pure as morning light,
Has watched the closing scene, and caught
  Inspiring visions from the sight.

Within her breast no passions rule,
  To mar the sweetness of her life ;
Her soul with love and truth so full,
  Bears her beyond a world of strife.

Yet on her brow there rests a care,
  She breathes it meekly in a sigh,
And carried in the evening air,
  It rises to the throne on high.

" Dear Lord of nature and of light,
  Whose name no mortal tongue can tell,
Thy works declare Thy power and might,
  For Thou dost order all things well.

To Thee the burden of my prayer,
  In simple faith I now present,
That Thou wouldst ease me of my care,
  And make me with my lot content.

D

My soul is burdened oft to know,
    What I may do to serve Thee, Lord :
And oh ! at times I tremble so,
    Lest I prove faithless to Thy Word.

I hear of many scattering seeds
    Of light and truth along the way ;
And I would too, in holy deeds,
    Serve Thee, dear Lord, from day to day.

What would'st Thou have me then to do ?
    Oh ! speak, relieve my anxious care ;
Give me a call to labour too,
    And in Thy vineyard do my share."

And while the maiden in her grief,
    Poured out her soul in secret prayer ;
There came a voice to her relief,
    And whispering in the evening air—

" Come be at rest, thou troubled one,
    And cease to entertain thy fears ;
With all thy doubts and cares have done,
    For ever wipe away thy tears.

The Lord in his own time will lead,
    And manifest His holy will ;
And that which He from thee doth need,
    Is to be patient and be still.

He knoweth what for thee is best,
    He only reaps where He hath sown.
In His infinite goodness rest,
    Let *love* instead of works atone."

RESIGNATION.

My way has been dark, and so little of light
　　Has beamed on my path ; the flowers never bloomed ;
My steps have been led thro' the darkness of night,
　　And clouds in the distance for ever have loom'd.

But why should my heart still with grief be oppressed,
　　Since friends whom I love, me with sympathy bear,
Or why, by deep sorrow my mind be distress'd,
　　While lov'd ones are willing my sorrow to share.

Oh ! 'tis heaven that gives to sorrow a balm,
　　And bathes the sad heart in the fountain of love,
Yes, 'tis heaven that sends the lov'd ones to calm
　　The rough billows of life, and raise us above.

The high waves of trouble with anger may roll,
　　And the great plain of life a desert may be,
And grief, she may taunt me, to weary my soul,
　　And the world may withhold its treasures from me.

Then as clouds of the morn let sadness depart,
　　Since the friends whom I love, prove constant and
　　　　true ;
I'll face the cold world with a nobler heart,
　　And I bid to my grief and my sorrows adieu.

DRIFT THOUGHTS.

MUST pain and grief, without relief,
  For ever be our portion here ?
Must friends betray, from day to day,
  And fail to be what they appear ?

Must selfish pride for ever ride
  With iron rule o'er humble life,
And thorns instead of roses spread,
  And peaceful mirth engender strife ?

Must love not last, when age has cast
  Upon the brow his silver'd threads ?
Must threescore years increase our fears
  Because the night its curtain spreads ?

Did heaven plan, for helpless man,
  A garden where no flowers grow ;
A desert wild, by sin defil'd
  A servitude of pain and woe ?

Some may give heed to such a creed,
  Or trust to chance, or reckless fate.
My faith is this, that heavenly bliss
  The earth shall yet illuminate.

That grief and pain shall cease to reign,
  When all fulfil the law of love,
And pride shall cease, and friends increase,
  When we reflect the light above.

Then turn the weed, and sow the seed,
  And heaven will cause the dew to fall ;
And so fulfil the higher will,
  Which labours for the good of all.

DISAPPOINTMENT.

How oft the dawn of opening day
  Is welcomed by a cloudless sky ;
But ere the morn has passed away
  The thunder shrouds are sweeping by.

So, like the sea, when all is calm,
  And tranquil lies its glassy breast,
The winds begin their mystic psalm,
  And turmoil reigns in place of rest.

The opening bud we so much prize,
  It promises a graceful bloom ;
But in its early effort dies,
  And fills the trusting heart with gloom.

Oh ! such is life. From youth to age
  'Tis nothing but a fitful scene.
Hope may awhile our woes assuage,
  And shield us from the dark unseen.

In simple youth we love and trust ;
  Oh ! sacred bliss ; in childhood's hours
We build our castle walls of dust,
  And strew our path with fancy flowers.

And though we lived a thousand years,
  So we would move from stage to stage.
The storms, the calms, the joys, the tears,
  They come alike for youth and age.

The early dawn, the peaceful wave,
  The opening bud, are emblems each,
And point to rest beyond the grave,
  Where disappointments never reach.

WOMAN RULES FOR A' THAT.

This world would be a dreary waste,
   And life a blank, and a' that,
If woman's charms could be effaced,
   Her winsome ways and a' that.
For a' that, and a' that,
   'Tis ordered so for a' that ;
Say what we may, she holds the sway,
   And right she should, for a' that.

Now, man may boast of wealth and kin,
   Of liberty, and a' that ;
Let Darwin trace his origin,
   He's but a slave for a' that.
For a' that, and a' that—
   Bogg'd and fogg'd, and a' that—
He's bound to play a second part
   Submissively, for a' that.

For honours on the battle field,
   In parliament, and a' that,
To woman first man has to yield,
   And knuckle down, and a' that.
For a' that, and a' that—
   'Tis surely true, for a' that—
Her smile is more than trophies won,
   Or fading wreaths, and a' that.

Her voice can still the troubled heart—
   Can spread dismay, and a' that ;
Her frown can make a nation smart,
   A Samson kneel, and a' that.
For a' that, and a' that,
   And " muckle mair " than a' that :
Her sceptre sways the universe
   For weal or woe, and a' that.

Men glory in their turret towers,
　　Their science, art, and a' that ;
Their larger gifts, and mental powers,
　　Their lords and peers, and a' that ;
For a' that, and a' that,
　　They're not supreme for a' that ;
A king may reign o'er Church and State,
　　But woman rules for a' that.

— — —

MY STAR.

A RADIANT star, an orb of light,
　　One, only one, 'mid thousands more,
　　That speak to me from yonder shore,
Is sacred to my thoughts to-night.

The clouds now drive across its course :
　　They're curling round and round in air ;
　　Their strange forms swinging everywhere,
Controlled by some unmeasured force.

The lonely shadows on the grass,
　　The bird that nestles on the tree,
　　The murmuring of the restless sea,
And vows that o'er my memory pass

Are sweetly dear—I know not why—
　　Nor may I risk a passing guess ;
　　Nor dare I for a reason press,
As something hidden ; let it lie.

No part of this strange scene ! I feel
　　To trespass on forbidden ground.
　　Like some untuned, unholy sound
My sigh is heard 'mid songs to steal.

I wait to sip the fragrant air ;
　To hold this ecstasy of thought,
　Which here to-night my soul has caught
From one dear star that glistens there.

KING FEAR.

AMONG the rulers, old King Fear
　Is monarch still of man and beast,
Lord of peasant, priest and peer,
　Master of the fast and feast.

The powers of earth may all combine,
　He meets their threats with sheer disdain ;
His sceptre renders each design
　A bane to those who spurn his reign.

Oh ! heartless tyrant ! Youth and Age
　Bear the dread shackles of thy state ;
The cradled babe, the hoary sage
　Alike own thee their potentate.

'Mid wrecks upon the stormy deep
　Thy fiendish laugh adds woe to grief ;
And when death shades begin to creep,
　All pay to thee thy final fief.

Relentless despot ! Prince of tears !
　When will thy potent terrors cease ?
When will the promised round of years
　Thy grasp from helpless man release ?

King Fear ! King Fear ! Oh, friendless foe !
　With less of tribute be content ;
Some portion of thy claim forego,
　And be not so on sorrow bent.

THE "MORE PORK" BIRD.

There is a wild bird in Australia resembling the English owl, the settlers call it the "More Pork," from its peculiar cry; it is heard only at night; it frequents the most lonely scrubs.

"More pork! More pork!" Who has not heard
The low, distant cry of the "more pork" bird?
When the twilight has passed and the evening come
The Australian sprite from wattle and gum
Flits in the dark. Then 'mid the oak trees
He answers the call which, borne on the breeze,
"More pork! More pork!" comes wafted along,
The mysterious wail of the wild bird's song.
The traveller rests in his lone bush camp
As he lists to the bells or his horse's tramp;
But the midnight watch from the old box-fork
Repeats his all's well, "More pork! More pork!"
He plays with the shadows which move on the plains,
And the hills wrapt in slumber give back his refrains;
But before the day dawns, his voice by degrees
Dies away in the distance among the scrub trees;
Like a "will-o'-the-wisp," he's not to be found,
For his power to elude he's become so renown'd;
Some say that he haunts the place of foul deeds,
And for just retribution to hidden guilt, pleads;
As an omen for evil by some he is blamed,
As a weatherwise prophet by all he is famed.
But be what he may, bird, prophet, or sprite,
On his mission unknown, a pilgrim by night,
He fulfils the high will 'mid darkness to work,
And wails through the night time, "More pork!
    More pork!"

A SONG.

Written for, and sung by the " LIGHT OF THE OCEAN " lodge of
Good Templars, composed of sailors of H.M.S. SAPPHO.

THE flag of dear Old England,
   The flag the captive frees;
" The flag that braved a thousand years
   The battle and the breeze."
That flag we honor here to-night,
   As British tars and true;
And hand in hand we pledge ourselves
   As allies of the blue.

CHORUS—Hurrah! hurrah! hurrah! hurrah!
   Then for the Temperance cause,
   And for the Sappho's crew—
   For they are here to-night my boys
   As allies of the blue.

On southern waves the Sappho rides,
   As firm a little craft
As e'er Port Jackson shelter gave,
   Or carried flag abaft.
Her skipper is as brave a tar
   As ever held a crew;
And we are here to-night my boys
   As allies of the blue.

CHORUS—Hurrah! &c.

Our hearts are stout as seamen's hearts,
   Warm as the mid-day sun;
And to defend your golden shores,
   Across the deep we've come.

The Union Jack proclaims the fact,
  That England's sons are true ;
So we are here to-night my boys
  As allies of the blue.

            CHORUS—Hurrah ! &c.

Your port a welcome to us gives,
  Its beauty stands supreme ;
And here we've found in kindred hearts
  True friendship's warmest gleam.
Our calling's on the mighty deep,
  To plough the ocean through ;
We're glad to be with you to-night
  As allies of the blue.

            CHORUS—Hurrah ! &c.

Oh ! sons of dear Old England,
  And daughters of the free,
From lessons of the past take heed,
  Awake ! awake, and see.
The foe that threatens now your homes
  Boasts still what he can do ;
But we have joined with heart and soul
  As allies of the blue.

            CHORUS—Hurrah ! &c.

No foreign power could ever stand
  Against the Saxon will ;
And we the Ocean Light have pledged
  To fight the battle till
The enemy within the camp
  Has found good cause to rue
That we did ever pledge ourselves
  As allies of the blue.

            CHORUS—Hurrah ! &c.

NATURE AND THE BROOK.

With wonder fill'd, I sit and rest
  Beside a lonely brook,
Whose little stream doth gently play,
And in its murmurs seems to say
  "Come read in nature's book."

So willingly my soul responds—
  I'll read thy simple tale,
That I may learn from thee to find
Sweet comfort for a troubled mind,
  And over grief prevail.

How long then, little brook, hast thou
  This silent shade possess'd ;
And who first mark'd thy course to run,
And shaded from the noon-day sun,
  Thy banks in verdure dress'd ?

And who gave thee thy power to flow,
  Desiring no repose ;
But gurgling on by day and night,
Thy crystal water sparkling bright,
  For ever onward flows.

I learn from thee that thou hast been
  For many ages past,
Conforming to the higher will,
To serve the higher purpose still
  And long as time shall last.

From thee may I fresh courage take,
  By faith abide my time,
And in the darkness and the light,
Pursue my way as in the sight
  Of nature's Lord and thine.

And may my inner life flow on,
   And gather day by day,
From showers descending from above,
The fulness of eternal love,
   To aid me on my way.

Then, little stream, my life shall flow
   Into eternal rest,
And all my wanderings then shall cease ;
No troubled wave shall harm my peace,
   Or sorrow move my breast.

——

A WELCOME TO CHRISTMAS.

COME, Christmas, merry Christmas ! now
   Smile on our youthful land ;
With Christmas bush bedeck thy brow
   And clasp Australia's hand.
Shake off thy chilly winter's guise
   And clothe thyself anew :
Come bask beneath our cloudless skies,
   Our skies of azure blue.

We welcome thee with heart and voice ;
   We hail thee, ancient friend,
And with thee once again rejoice
   While lights and shadows blend.
Old memories now of bygone days
   Are mingling with the new.
We chant the Young World's Christmas lays
   As loyal, warm, and true
As those our honor'd fathers sang
   In happy days of yore,
Or from the bells of England rang,
   Those bells of ancient lore.

ON A BUTTERFLY.

YONDER on a lily white,
  Rests a lovely butterfly,
Basking in the morning light,
Ready for its maiden flight,
  Spreading out its wings to dry.

Yesternight a chrysalis,
  Strangely fashion'd helpless thing;
Now 'tis in the midst of bliss,
Waiting for a sunbeam's kiss,
  Ere it ventures on the wing.

What a world of pure surprise
  Opens to its early view!
What a field of pleasure lies
Stretched before its wondering eyes,
  While it sips the morning dew!

Is the past forgotten?   All
  Its wanderings when a worm?
Does its memory recall
How it wove its funeral pall,
  To serve its chrysalis term?

Once it crept upon the leaf,
  Now that trembles 'neath its weight,
Seeking from the storm relief,
Or while hiding as a thief,
  Like some thing inanimate.

Has a new creation wrought,
  Out of darkness, purer light?
Has a new-born vision brought
All its former life to naught,
  Turning morning into night.

How its rainbow sails unfold!
   See! they bend upon the breeze,
Over rose and marigold,
O'er the bower and o'er the wold,
   Soaring over rocks and trees.

O'er the brook so calm and still,
   Where the little streamlet plays,
Darting over mead and rill,
Joy and pleasure at its will;
   What a change from former days!

When we drop this mortal weight,
   Learning what it is to die;
When we leave this chrysalis state,
And the union terminate.
   And the dust with dust shall lie—

Will probation have an end?
   When this dream-state is o'er
Will the soul in bliss ascend
And will joy and sorrow blend
   In that region never more?

———— —

THE CREED OF THE BIGOT.

    I hold to the faith
      Of my Fathers before me;
    At the altar they rear'd,
      I bow still and pray;
    Their blood-spangled banner
      Is still waving o'er me;
    Their creed of "Sheer Force"
      I swear by to day.

FAITH.

" Let each keep to their own spheres and do their work therein.
Christianity has no weapons in her original armoury which can be
wielded against science, and science cannot attack spiritual truths
with purely intellectual weapons.   No one asks for a spiritual proof
that the earth goes round the sun ; it is equally absurd to ask for a
purely intellectual proof of the existence of an all-loving Father.
And it would be wiser if science kept her hands off Christianity.
Mankind will bear a great deal, but it will not long bear the denial of
a God of Love, the attempt to thieve away the hope of being perfect
and our divine faith in immortality.   These things are more precious
than all physical discoveries."—STOPFORD A. BROOKE.

IT is the faith which works by love
    That conquers every fear,
And lifts the drooping heart above
    The doubts which haunt it here.

Our subtle forms of reason give
    No comfort to the soul ;
They offer no alternative—
    Than earth, no brighter goal.

Law guides the destinies of worlds,
    And finds each star its place ;
But Faith, which works by love, unfolds
    The mysteries of grace.

By law we measure earth and sea—
    Yet law cannot atone ;
'Tis the unchangeable decree
    To reap what we have sown.

Law fills the soul with fear and dread
    And veils the heavenly light ;
But loving Faith can glory shed
    Amid the darkest night.

No grasp of intellect can span
    What Faith alone reveals;
No form of creeds can give to man
    What Heaven from man conceals.

It is the Faith that works by love,
    And not by slavish fear,
That lifts the longing soul above
    The doubts which haunt it here.

———

WRITTEN IN A BIRTHDAY TEXT-BOOK,

CALLED "LINKS OF MEMORY."

To Miss K. E. H.

KIND memories dwell
Amid these pages lowly.
To thee, dear friend,
Each loving link is holy;
Each breathes a spell.
How long? alas! how long?
All earthly links are breaking,
Rest not thy heart!
Beyond these hills
Unbroken day is waking;
There links can never part,
There friendship has no ending.

E

THE ILLUSION.

[We were to have met Miss —— at the rafting ground, where she was to join the party at 8 a.m., but unfortunately she mistook the path and reached a point on the river bank some two miles further up. On our return home, we thought it well to search again for our missing friend.   A faint coo-ey in the distance encouraged our search.]

SHE waited by the river brink,
　　And shaded by the wild oak trees
She listless watched the swallows drink
　　Before they soar'd upon the breeze.

On every leaf the early dew,
　　Like emeralds, glistened in the shade,
While lovely morning stayed and threw
　　A magic spell o'er hill and glade.

The rippling of the golden stream,
　　The music in the boughs above,
To her were like a pleasant dream—
　　A pleasant dream of early love,

An interval of conscious rest,
　　A foretaste of a happier sphere ;
It lull'd awhile her aching breast,
　　And brought the land of glory near.

The balmy moments flitted past,
　　The leafless trunks then mock'd her fears ;
And long gaunt shadows fell, and cast
　　Their cheerless forms like fun'ral biers.

" When will they come ?   I hear the oar !
　　The merry laugh !   They come, I hear !"
Alas ! 'twas fancy—nothing more ;
　　'Twas fancy mock'd her willing ear.

The swallows, on their homeward flight,
　Again came skipping o'er the wave ;
The emerald drops are gone, and Night
　Is sitting on yon lonely grave.

The river flows ; she hears it say,
　As round its slimy bank it curls,
" The peaceful morn has passed away,
　And now my death-cold shroud unfurls."

Has fancy dull'd her wayward brain ?
　Or fear her anxious mind possess'd—
Again, she hears the laugh ; again,
　Again, she hears the waters press'd.

" When will they come ?　Can they forget
　That on the river brink I wait ?
They, too, must know the sun has set,
　And I might meet some cruel fate.

" The winding path, through brush and fern,
　I dare not trust by evening shades,
I could not find the forest turn
　Before the last of twilight fades.

" When will they come ? See yonder star !
　So lonely in that deep abyss !
My only hope is not so far
　Beyond my reach, ah, no ! as this.

" God of the broken-hearted ! Thou
　Canst speed the little boat to save.
I hear ! It comes ! I see it now ;
　It glides upon the starlit wave."

"IN ESSENTIALS UNITY, IN NON-ESSENTIALS LIBERTY, IN ALL THINGS CHARITY."

" BELIEVE and live ! " so say the numerous sects ;
" Believe and live," no honest heart objects.
But what believe ? and who shall draw the line ?
Or who the limits of our faith define ?
All plead their claims from Apostolic lore,
And some attached to this have something more.

Rome takes her stand, brands every doubt a sin,
Trusts sacrificial acts the goal to win ;
Binds every conscience by the " Church decrees,"
Then bolts the heavenly gates with Peter's keys.

The " Church of England " next, with broader bands,
Will lay alone on those its " holy hands "
Who to the Thirty-nine give full consent,
And stand aloof in righteous self-content.
Divided into High and Low and Broad,
While groaning 'neath the Ritualistic rod.

Then Methodists to Orthodoxy wed,
Must have the flock by class experience fed.
Renounce old Rome, and Rome reformed impeach,
Reject John Calvin, but John Wesley preach.

" Independents," if not in deed, in name,
Though not to Wesley bound, hold much the same ;
They never meet in " class," each church alone
Forms its own laws, no other can disown.

The " Church of Scotland " differs from the rest—
Still holds its ancient formula the test
Of who are not, and who are " gau'n the road,"
Despite the " broad Kirk " views of good McLeod ;
Too lax of law they judge their fellow-men,
And fain the *Decalogue* would teach again.

With all the Baptist differs. How could he
With those who sprinkle babes in faith agree ?
So much he sees in this one act comprised,
To all he cries, " Repent and be baptized ! "

For this, as well as other ancient rites
To bind the faith, the minor satellites
'Mid strong contentions, strive to hold their place,
And call their types and forms "*The Means of Grace.*"

The " Plymouth Brethren," to the letter bound,
Expectant wait to hear the trumpet sound,
When the Elect shall rise to life again,
To usher in the long " millenial reign."

Then, much esteemed, the followers of Fox,
By one and all regarded heterodox ;
They fix their faith in no external rite,
But base their creed on " Universal light."

Now, all the sects to differ should agree.
Loose their own bonds, then set their neighbours free ;
Take one pure life a model for the rest,
Accept the Creedless Creed, the only test.

As trees are known by fruits, so judge by deeds,
For holy lives accept not verbal creeds ;
The dying thief had only one short plea :
" When in Thy kingdom, Lord, remember me."

MARY OF MAGDALA.

MARK that poor wandering Magdalen !
Whose soul is stirr'd by holy thought,
For whom the Mystery has wrought
Deliverance from the bonds of sin.

Her dismal night is turned to day,
   The burden of her guilt is moved,
   Before high heaven she stands approved;
'Tis little what the rabble say!

She spurns the lewd and hollow jest,
   The meanful smile, the taunt and jeer,
   For "perfect love" has conquered fear,
And lull'd her troubled mind to rest.

To Simon's house she bends her way;
   Has summon'd courage to intrude;
   Her heart o'erflows with gratitude,
For all she's heard the prophet say.

Now stooping o'er the heav'nly guest,
   Her tears fall fast, they fall and meet,
   And mingle on the sacred feet,
While doubts revolve in Simon's breast.

There sits the model Pharisee!
   The prototype of all his kind!
   Traditions have obscured his mind;
He fails the *in*wrought good to see.

In ceremonial law well versed;
   The straitest of the strictest sect;
   A son of Abraham! elect!
While she, "without the pale," is curs'd.

" Is this the prophet long foretold,
   Who takes this outcast sinner's kiss—
   The true Messiah—and can this
Be he, in whom we shall behold

"The likeness of the Father's face,
   'The Word in flesh made manifest,'
   To whom the Patriarchs confess'd;
The great deliverer of our race?

" It cannot be ! or he would greet
  This Magdalen in her despair,
  Who dares, with her dishevell'd hair,
To dry the tear-drops on his feet,

" With righteous wrath." So Simon spoke,
  And reason'd in his icy soul ;
  Thus he interpreted the scroll,
Till light upon his vision broke.

So zealous for Mosaic rule,
  He hardly saw how truth and grace
  Could sacrificial rites replace,
And bring deliverance free and full.

Oh ! blessed truth, the Word from heaven ;
  Love redeems where *law* must blast,
  And every stricken soul at last
May *go in peace and be forgiven.*

"AND THUS THE WORLD GOES ROUND."

(A SONG.)

THAT ancient man did truly say,
That " grief was portioned out to all,
    Both rich and poor ; "
Like him, I've journeyed on life's way
A pilgrim, seeking day by day
    A shade secure ;
But earth affords no place of rest,
And they alone are surely blest
    Who live to love,
For Heaven this power has kindly given
    To lead our souls above.

In youth we're prone to lean upon
The reeds of life, and fix our trust
  In treasures vain ;
So when our early years have run,
There's much we find must be undone,
  We wisdom gain ;
But when old age and silver'd locks,
Have done their work, we see the rocks
  Where danger lay,
And thus we learn in life's great school,
  Our lessons day by day.

True happiness is found in Love ;
Where love is pure 'tis Heaven below ;
  And this I've found.
All earthly treasures are as dust,
They suffer loss from moth and rust,
  But love's abound ;
'Tis folly then to grieve and chime
About the things that change with Time
  And cannot last ;
At best, Life's but a passing scene
  In which our lot is cast.

That ancient man who heard the sod
Upon my loved sire's coffin drop,
  He, too, has gone ;
His honest heart now beats no more,
For Death's cold hand has barr'd the door,
  He's journeyed on :
Though Fortune never smiled on him
He had a noble soul within.
  And this I've found—
We leave Life's drama each in turn,
  And thus the world goes round.

THE DESERTED WIFE'S APPEAL.

(A SONG.)

I ONCE was happy, blithe, and gay—
    Pleased with life's passing toys ;
Youth drove the fear of care away,
    And strew'd my path with joys.
I trusted all who promised fair,
    To all my heart was free ;
But never dream'd a hidden snare
    Was on the path for me.

My life was as the golden dawn
    Before the opening day ;
Dark clouds soon gather'd, and the morn
    Drove all my joys away.
Oh, sad the change ! now wild despair
    Instead of youthful glee ;
Who ever dream'd a hidden snare
    Was on the path for me ?

'Twas not his heart that went astray :
    No, it was kind and brave ;
'Twas in the cup the venom lay—
    The power to enslave.
He would not heed my earnest prayer
    To stay his liberty ;
He never dreamed a hidden snare
    Was on the path for me.

Now all is dark ! 'Mid pain and grief
    I'm friendless and forlorn;
Oh ! bring me for my babe relief ;
    Alas that it was born !
Ah ! who will now my sorrow share ?
    And who my helper be ?
Did any dream a hidden snare
    Was on the path for me ?

THE EREMITE.

WITH the wattle boughs I've built my bower,
  Near the bend where the river turns,
Where the wild bees seek the native flower,
And the trees grow high 'neath the clear blue sky
  And shade the fronded ferns.

Behind the dark hills the sun has now set,
  And the cool eventide has come ;
The brightness of day is lingering yet,
While the mountain height, for a beacon light,
  Guides the poor shepherd home.

The leaves as they fall are borne by the tide,
  One by one they're wafted along,
Like my round of years which so swiftly glide,
On the stream of life, to the ocean's strife,
  To mingle with the throng.

The deep river flows, and leads me to think
  Of the days which have long since past ;
And from my bower, while over the brink
I gaze on the stream, as one in a dream,
  Whose lot's in sorrow cast.

So lonely and sad, I list to the wind,
  As it moans like some restless sprite
Among the oak boughs, while seeking to find
Some soul to distress, some heart to oppress,
  In some poor eremite.

Oh, river so cold ! flow on in thy course !
  Day and night have no change for thee ;
Thy heart cannot know the pangs of remorse,
No longings for rest can weary thy breast,
  Or change thy destiny.

THE GRAVE BY THE SHORE.

ALONE in the bright moonlight reclining,
    I list to the murmuring deep;
And the stars far above me are shining,
    While the rocks unconsciously sleep.
Silver moonbeams are skipping and playing,
    Like nymphs on the white-crested waves,
And the zephyrs around me are swaying,
    The willows that weep by the graves.
But I join in the wail of the murmuring sea,
While I mourn o'er the lost one who never can be,
On the earth, what she once was, a solace to me,
    The love of my earlier days.

'Gainst the rocks the proud breakers are beating,
    They veil the rude cliff with their spray;
On the beach the wild curlew is greeting,
    And calling his comrades away.
'Neath the moonlight the sea-gull is sleeping,
    On the wave-worn flag by the shore,
And the limpet is stealthily creeping,
    Alone on its moss-cover'd floor.
But my soul it is filled with a heavenly glow,
And some spirit I fancy is waiting to know,
If the one whom I lov'd in the days long ago
    Still dwells in my heart as before.

The wild oaks in the wind are repining,
    They bend their frail tops to the breeze;
And the clouds with their silvery lining,
    In the moonlight are floating at ease;
And the lights 'mid the shadows are gleaming,
    Far in the rock-sheltered cave,

While now of a lost one I am dreaming
 By the willows that weep o'er her grave.
But the moon is declining far off in the west,
And she sleeps by the sea shore in unbroken rest,
Still she dwells in my heart as a heavenly guest,
 While willows weep over her grave.

———

"WHAT SHALL THE HARVEST BE?"

On! what shall the harvest be
 For those who sow in tears ?
Oh ! what shall the harvest be
 When harvest time appears?

When all the toil has ended,
 And fallow ground repays
The labour we expended
 'Mid long and dreary days ?

Then with the song and chorus,
 We'll reap the golden ears,
And join with those before us
 Who till'd the ground in tears.

We sow to reap in gladness
 When reaping time shall come ;
We sow in grief and sadness
 Before we journey home.

We sow in storm and sunshine,
 We'll reap 'mid heavenly calm ;
We work to rest at eve-time,
 And then we'll bear the palm.

THE LADY'S REPLY TO THE GIPSY.

(A SONG.)

WARNING Gipsy ! I did trust him,
　Fearing not thy mystic wand,
And before the sacred altar,
　Pledg'd to him my heart and hand ;
I was young, and fair, and gentle,
　As a flower in Paradise,
But I heeded not thy warning,
　Or thy fears, nor thy advice.

Grey with sorrow, now my tresses
　So bespeak the years of care,
Blighted hopes and vows soon broken,
　Bow my heart in wild despair.
Life which was to me a garden,
　Now is like the desert plain,
Joy has given place to mourning,
　And can ne'er return again.

Full my cup, and sad my lot is,
　Lingering thro' the weary day,
Would that dark-eyed stranger never
　Led my simple heart away.
Gipsy, tell me where I comfort
　Now may find in my sad woe ;
Will the clouds around me darken,
　Shall my sorrow deeper flow ?

Must the silent grave receive me,
　Ere my troubled heart's at peace ?
Tell me, tell me, Gipsy, kindly
　Pity ! cause my grief to cease.
" I did pray thee and entreat thee,
　Gentle lady ! much I mourn,
I can only point to danger,
　And against deceivers warn.

" Riches lost may be regather'd,
    Even health may be regained,
Early love may be rekindled,
    And youth's follies be restrained ;
But the altar binds for ever,
    Death alone can break the bond ;
Thou didst trust him, hapless lady,
    And despis'd the Gipsy's wand !"

THE CHANGELESS FRIEND.

(A HYMN.)

THERE is no change, O Lord, in Thee ;
    The hills shall crumble and decay,
    And all that's seen shall pass away,
But Thou the same must ever be,
There is no change, O Lord, in Thee.

From age to age Thou art the same ;
    The princes of this world shall fall,
    The high, the low, the great and small,
Must bow before Thy changeless name ;
From age to age Thou art the same.

Thy mercies are for ever sure,
    For like Thyself they ever last,
    When all our earthly joys are past
They cannot cease—they shall endure ;
Thy mercies are for ever sure.

The weary find in Thee a rest,
    The broken hearted find relief
    In Thee, from all their bitter grief,
For all mankind in Thee are blest ;
The weary find in Thee a rest.

There is no change, O Lord, in Thee,
　The first and last, the King of kings ;
　The creature and created things
May wane and die and cease to be,
There is no change, O Lord, in Thee.

THE SONG OF THE STOCKMAN.

I LOVE the romance of a wild bush life
　'Mong the Alps of a southern sphere ;
With " billy " and " weed " and the camp sheath knife,
A steed of true blood for fire or flood,
　And an honest comrade's cheer.

" Charms of the city !" what are they beside
　The romance of my rough slab home,
Near the scrub-bound creek, where wallabies hide,
Where the kangaroo and the lone curlew,
　On the mountain passes roam.

Where the emu strides on the treeless plain
　In the pride of his native speed,
Where the dingo hunts, but oft hunts in vain,
The neighbouring wood for stolen food,
　And bears and opossums feed.

Who choose may dwell in the glitter and glare
　And the noise of the bustling town,
But give me my hut and the mountain air,
With the fleecy flock and the grazing stock
　On the rich and verdant down !

" Position and wealth !" I covet them not,
　For honors I never did crave,
With little content—man's happiest lot
Is living to love, and soaring above
　Humanity's restless wave.

TO THE HERO OF THE "LOCH ARD."

During a gale in 1878 the "Loch Ard" was lost off Cape Otway.
Midshipman Thomas Pearce, after reaching the shore, heard the
cry of Eveline Carmichael while clinging to a portion of the wreck.
He again faced the surging waves and brought her safely to land.
They were the only survivors.

WHERE the sunken rocks defy,
And the dead enshrouded lie
    As ocean guests,
Where the waves in mountains rise,
And the dark clouds hide the skies,
    The "Loch Ard" rests.

Where the rude and rugged walls
Catch the snow-white spray that falls
    As bridal veils,
Where the breakers ceaseless roar,
And the foaming billows pour,
    And tempest wails,

There old Neptune's gallant son,
Fearless, fought with death, and won
    Fair Eveline ;
From the deep he heard her cry,
Bravely for her dared to die
    Unsung, unseen.

Battled with the curling deep,
Where the fierce winds angry sweep
    O'er coral graves ;
Nobly bore her to the beach,
Laid her safe beyond the reach
    Of angry waves.

Seal'd the high and rocky steeps
Where the lonely eagle sleeps,
 The feather'd chief ;
Found the shepherd's winding track,
Brought the welcome tidings back,
 And staid her grief.

Let the Victor's praise be sung,
Let a fadeless wreath be hung
 Around his name.
Hero of the lost " Loch Ard,"
Take thy merited reward,
 Immortal fame.

AN ODE TO

AUSTRALIA.

FAIR daughter of Britain, I will cherish thy name ;
In the notes which are sweetest in sadness,
I will sing of my fair island home.
Thy glens and fern bowers so enchant me,
And thy blue shrouded mountains so stately,
Oh ! they tell me that glory awaits thee,
That garlands are wreathed for thy brow.
Australia ! thy children delight in thy beauty,
O'er thy hills and thy valleys kind nature has strewn
Her rich bounties so freely,
And formed thee a fair Eden for man.
Oh ! home of all lands, so endearing,
From afar may no dark clouds be nearing,
To check the fair bloom of thy youth,
Or tarnish thy unsullied name.
May thy banner of blue by no foe be degraded,
Nor thy fair sons and daughters for dishonor upbraided
Nor thy harp on the willow be hung.

THE LOST MUSE.

In vain I seek my early muse,
  When lonely murmuring streamlets meet,
Where wild birds sip the morning dews,
  And hills are mark'd by fairy feet.

Where sleeping pebbles 'neath the stream,
  That shine like many colour'd beads,
Have smiled to mock me in my dream,
  While peeping through the curling weeds.

I wander by the fern-lined caves,
  And 'mid the gum and wattle groves ;
Down rocky cliffs to restless waves,
  That ceaseless wail among the coves.

And now I list to hear the " Bell,"
  The " Coachman " and the sad curlew,
And by the brook that laves the dell.
  I wait the fall of evening dew.

In moon-lit bowers alone I've sighed,
  To feel her near me once again,
To love and woo her by my side,
  I've longed, but oh ! I've longed in vain.

Some reckless act, perchance, of mine,
  Has grieved my muse's purer thought,
Some loveless word, some soulless line,
  Alas ! has this estrangement wrought.

And now I sing discordant chimes,
  Discordant chimes without relief ;
My thoughts are clothed in broken rhymes,
  So strangely mixed with love and grief.

"HE WIPES THE TEAR FROM EVERY EYE."

WHEN troubles like the waters meet,
  And angry waves are raging high,
Then raise thy heart in prayer to Him;
  He wipes the tear from every eye.

When of thy loving friend bereft,
  And clouds of darkness hide the sky,
Then let thy prayer to Him ascend;
  He wipes the tear from every eye.

FRIENDSHIP.

WRITTEN FOR MISS C. B. H.'S ALBUM.

FRIENDS are but blossoms on life's stream,
They charm us for a time, then seem
  To fill our hearts with sadness.
Like sweetest melodies, they leave
Us vainly longing, then deceive
  With spectral hopes for gladness.

They move and flit like Elmo's light,
And glitter to our dazzled sight
  As angels of the morning.
They come and go as fairy flowers;
They pass forgotten, sunny showers!
  Alas! they leave us mourning.

God only knows why all our joys,
Are nothing more than painted toys,
  Or shadows on a river.
He, only He, alone can know
Why we must part with all below,
  And why true friendships sever.

But ah ! my loved and valued friend,
Believe me, I do not intend
　　To speak of friendship vainly.
I simply place a poet's thought
Upon this page, sad years have taught,
　　Forgive me, if too plainly.

————— ——

TO A YOUNG BRIDE.

DEAR friend of my youth may thy home ever be
Of all spots upon earth the dearest to thee,
May heaven's choice blessing descend from above—
A dove on the Ark with a message of love.

May the Heavenly visitant never depart,
But remain through life's term to comfort thy heart,
And be unto you each the sure link to bind
In truth and affection each mind unto mind.

The storm-clouds of life in their order will lower,
And thy dearest hope may fade as a flower,
But bow to the storm till the darkness be pass'd ;
No grief nor deep sorrow for ever can last.

Could I purchase my wish thy steps would be led
Through the garden of life where the flowers are spread
No foe should distress thee or cause thee alarm,
The Sword and the Angel should shield thee from harm,

The cold world should bring thee no trials nor tears,
Thy joys should increase with the roll of the years,
The bright visions of life should never entomb
Their brightness and lustre in sorrow or gloom.

I would wish from my heart all trouble should cease
And thy home be the home of the heav'nly peace.

IMPROMPTU LINES.

At Wiseman's Ferry, on the Hawkesbury River, the walls of one of the oldest colonial churches are standing. It was liberally endowed by Mr. WISEMAN, whose remains are enclosed in a leaden coffin which to-day may be seen through the iron grating beneath the stone floor.

A roofless church, where " curlews " keep
A midnight watch, while coffins sleep
   Beneath the sacred floor ;
Where once the old kirk parson spread,
His holy hands o'er WISEMAN's head
   And bade him rise no more.

THE COMMISSIONED OFFICER.

Addressed to "His Reverence" Charles Francis Peter Collingridge, Gaol Chaplain, who protested against my lectures to the prisoners, on the ground that I was not " A Commissioned Officer."

I ASK your reverence, Charley dear,
Just lend me, for a while, your ear,
While I approach in " pious fear "
   A true " commissioned officer."

I know 'tis very hard for you
To serve the State and LEO too ;
You surely have your work to do
   As a commissioned officer.

You say your care for souls is great,
God help the poor at heaven's gate
If you stand there to hold the plate,
   A true commissioned officer.

Oh ! Charley, think of days gone by,
When on the flames the piercing cry
Ascended to the One on high—
　"Spare the commissioned officers."

Thank God, we breathe a freer air,
And for the future don't despair,
Although you hold the chaplain's chair,
　The true commissioned officer.

We are by one sure guide advised
To prove and test the "authorised:"
That guide, dear Francis, you despised
　As a commissioned officer.

What would He say to you, who took
The Scribes and Pharisees to book,
And spurned the proud and saintly look
　Of all "commissioned" officers.

Do you expect hard hearts to touch
By mildly mumbling double Dutch ?
Oh ! heaven preserve us all from such
　Divine commissioned officers.

If it be true that God does send
The likes of you our souls to mend,
A compliment He must intend
　All non-commissioned officers.

Was ever there such balderdash
As saving sinners' souls for cash ?
Shame to the State that pays for trash
　And such commissioned officers.

Now, your reverence, ere I close,
One thing to you let me propose,
But from my cheek pray don't suppose
　I'm a commissioned officer.

You are responsible, you say,
For those who at your altar pray
(If one to hell should find his way)
    As a commissioned officer.

Now, Frank, if all you teach be true,
That God "requires these souls of you,"
I fear the de'il will well tattoo
    His own commissioned officer.

Since your own sins you have to bear,
Your reverence, sure 'twould not be fair
That you should have another's share
    As a commissioned officer.

Escape the risk, and sure 'tis great,
Your own soul mend ere 'tis too late,
Then you may pass at heaven's gate
    As a commissioned officer.

Oh ! so much depends
On the choice of one's friends,
    With this I'm sure you'll agree.
I've found in my day
'Tis wiser to stay
    Before you're familiar and free.

But once having found,
By testing the ground
    On which your friendship will stand,
That everything's square—
Conditions being fair—
    Withhold not your heart, nor your hand.

TO MISS ———

THESE lines shall seek no higher place
   Than on this yellow tinted page,
A simple epitaph to trace
   The windings of a bygone age.

When you then gambolled on the lawn,
   And happy, lisped your girlish lay ;
But I had entered on the dawn
   Of op'ning manhood's early day.

I would not, if I could, forget
   Those loveful, blissful days of yore ;
And though so many suns have set,
   Their memory brightens more and more.

They've pass'd like blossoms on a stream,
   Whose fragrance pleased me for a time ;
But, oh ! they haunt me as a dream,
   Or like some long-remembered chime.

ON THE DEATH OF AN OLD
NEWFOUNDLAND DOG.

POOR Captain's dead ! he bowed his head,
   His troubles are over now ;
No plumes were spread, no prayers were read,
   When he gave his last " bow-wow."

Though up in years, he shed no tears
    When told his end was nearing;
He knew no fears, and stood the jeers
    Of the other curs while teazing.

To Rover's care he left a share
    Of all his goods and chattels,
For Monkey's fare he left the hair
    He cast in all his battles.

Of good degree poor dog was he,
    His bosom friend was Ponto,
Of all the three, he grieved to see
    His bosom friend sool'd on to.

He did not fail to wag his tail
    When Puss and Tom approached him,
And did they ail, his ancient wail
    Did always comfort bring them.

Of troubles, too, he had a few,
    The " sparrows " found their victim,
They ever knew, the poor old screw
    Might scratch, but could not shift them.

Of later days, his doggish ways
    Demanded speedy action,
The debt he pays, the call obeys,
    To nature's satisfaction.

So all is o'er, and he's no more
    With bones and scraps delighting;
The sea will roar, just as before,
    And fleas will go on biting.

THE PARTING.

We stood by the little garden gate,
  And the moments glided by,
While the pale moon shone above our heads,
  Far up in the distant sky.
The bright stars peeped from their lonely homes,
  Through the clouds that coursed along, -
And the wind was murmuring through the trees
  In a sweet and plaintive song.
From sleeping flowers the dew-drops hung,
  And tipped with silvery light,
The shadows played upon one path,
  On that calm December night.

We stood by the little garden gate,
  Beneath the flowering vine,
He whispered a hope, an earnest prayer,
  As he placed his hand in mine;
He whisper'd a hope that God above
  Would lovingly cast in one,
And bind by a changeless link our lives,
  Till the sands of life were run.

He spoke of a better time to come,
  And the Father's ceaseless care,
Of that trust that measures not His love,
  Of his judgments, just and fair,
Of the Light that lights the darkest heart,
  In spite of a life of sin,
Of joys that flow from the heav'nly hills.
  And the Word that dwells within.

But I fancy still I hear his voice ;
   In my happy dreams I see
The fence and the little garden gate
   Where he pledged his love to me,
The winding path and the trellised vine,
   I fancy I see them yet.
His last " good-bye "—and the kiss he gave,
   Oh ! I never can forget.

———

'TIS BUT A WILD ROSE.

(A SONG).

'TIS but a wild rose
   In a letter for me,
From a hand so gentle and fair ;
   'Tis pressed on a word,
   Which I only may see ;
It is tied with her brown silken hair.

The letter is soiled
   By the dear little flow'r ;
It's fragrance has pass'd on the air.
   She pull'd it for me,
   In a wild fairy bow'r ;
It is tied with her brown silken hair.

It whispers a name
   Which I dare not repeat,
I would though to you if I dare,
   A love thought, it rests
   In its beauty, complete ;
It is tied with her brown silken hair.

THE YOUNG MOTHER'S LULLABY.

THE sun has set behind the hills,
    And shadows softly creep
Over the dark, dark ocean waves,
    Over the restless deep.
Night's curtain now is falling fast,
    And Nature calls to rest,
Come, lay thee down, my darling babe,
    Sweet birdie in thy nest.

      Sleep, darling, sleep—no harm is near,
        Thy mother guards thy bed ;
      Sleep, darling, sleep—the angels, dear,
        Are hovering o'er thy head.

Come, rest thee now, my cherub, rest,
    Fold down thy silken hair,
And let me kiss thy rosy cheek,
    And breathe my evening prayer.
The stars are peeping through the clouds,
    That sail across the sky,
To hear thy mother sing to thee
    Her first sweet lullaby.

      Sleep, darling, sleep—no harm is near,
        Thy mother guards thy bed ;
      Sleep, darling, sleep—the angels, dear,
        Are hovering o'er thy head.

A HAPPY NEW YEAR.

"I wish you a Happy New Year,"
　　I'm tired of this fulsome expression,
We use it sometimes to appear,
　　And be on the tip-toe of fashion.

But let it be so if it may,
　　This time I wish it so dearly,
For a Happy New Year I pray ;
　　For you, Annie, I wish it sincerely.

A TRIBUTE TO MY MOTHER.

An aged "Friend," a quaker dame
　　Whose bond was ever "yea or nay,"
Who knew her, kindly spoke her name,
　　And bade her, with a smile, "good day."
　　　　A woman loved—of Christian fame,
　　　　Clad meekly in her "quaker grey."

A woman mark'd among the crowd,
　　With thoughtful brow, and snow-white hair ;
Not stately in her mien, but bowed
　　With years of grief, which none could share.
　　　　To tell her sorrows ! far too proud,
　　　　Her life was one unbroken prayer.

www.ingramcontent.com/pod-product-compliance
Lightning Source LLC
Chambersburg PA
CBHW032154010726
47493CB00008BA/2698